PRESENTED BY

Mark Thompson

THE CHURCH MICE AND THE MOON

Graham Oakley

ATHENEUM NEW YORK

J
Easy
Oakley

17030

Early one Friday afternoon, Arthur and Humphrey, the leaders of the church mice, were strolling in the churchyard grumbling about how small the portions of pudding had been at lunch. Humphrey was saying that prominent members of society, like themselves, should have double helpings and Arthur was agreeing and saying that somebody should do something about it when suddenly . . .

. . . they saw something that made them think that somebody *had* done something about it.

FROM A
DEVOTED
ADMIRER

BEST LEMON
AND CURRANT
CHEESECAKE

WELC...

But they didn't think so for very long.

They let out such a mighty squeak that all the other mice, who had been lounging about gossiping, came running up to see what all the fuss was about.

And Sampson, the church cat, who had been enjoying a good scratch in the porch, came running up, too. They were just in time to see a van go hurtling up the street.

The mice all started wailing and wringing their paws and moaning about how Arthur and Humphrey were gone for ever and ever. They made such a racket that if Sampson's mind hadn't been occupied, he might have forgotten his vow of brotherly love towards mice. But his mind was occupied, and it was the strange word that he'd seen on the back of the van that occupied it.

"WOMUMP," he said thoughtfully and rather loudly. The mice stopped twittering and got ready to run because they thought he'd suddenly gone funny in the head due to all the excitement.

"To solve a crime you've got to have a clue, and WOMUMP is a clue," Sampson went on. "Find WOMUMP and you've found those two silly mice, and I know just where to begin the search." Then he said something about it being elementary, my dear Watson, to a mouse whose name he knew quite well wasn't Watson, and hurried off.

When the mice were sure his back was turned, they all looked at one another and tapped their foreheads knowingly, but they followed him just the same.

Sampson knew that the river which flowed past the church was called the Lugg, so he reasoned that if he went either up-stream or down-stream he would eventually come to Clodbury-on-Lugg. He went up-stream because the scenery was prettier that way.

He found what he wanted without any bother, and, as there was still an hour or two until tea time, he decided to start his investigation there and then. So he sent the mice back to the vestry, where they lived, because they would only get under foot. Then he set off on his search.

It did seem an awful long way. He thought to himself, "Missing tea for the sake of friendship is one thing, but missing tea *and* supper is another," and he was on the point of turning back and leaving the mice to sort out their problems by themselves, when he saw the signboard.

So he decided that he might just as well carry on with his search as he was on the spot. He had no trouble getting into the place because the guard really didn't have things very well organized.

And once in, he found his friends in no time at all.

The poor mice were having a terrible time. They cheered
up a bit when they saw Sampson . . .

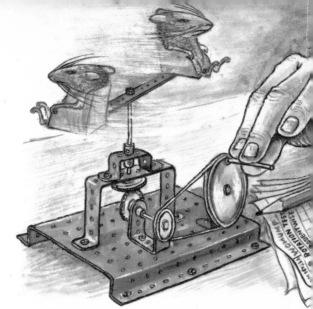

. . . but it's very difficult to stay cheered u
when you're being rotated, oscillated . . .

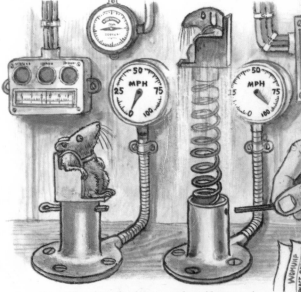

. . . accelerated, gyrated, vibrated and
undulated, even if it is for the sake of
Progress.

They might not have been very cheerful, but they were very puzzled. They knew they were being made into astronauts, but they weren't quite sure what an astronaut was. Humphrey said that a friend of his knew somebody who had read in a newspaper that somebody on the telly had said that an astronaut was a camel with three humps. But they didn't see how rotating and gyrating and doing huge horrible sums would turn them into one of those.

When the scientists had run out of nasty things to do, they went, leaving a pile of books which, they said, the mice had to read from beginning to end before they got a bite of supper.

Sampson watched all these goings on in a terrible rage. "They may only be mice," he said to himself, "but even mice have feelings. I've never treated mice as badly as that, and I've had the excuse of being a cat." Still, there was nothing he could do for his friends until morning, so he made a quick tour of the grounds and then looked for a nice warm place to curl up in for the night.

He soon found one, though there wasn't much room in it at first because it was full of wires. But after he had disconnected them all, it was just big enough for him to creep into and make himself snug and cosy.

CAUTION
AUTOMATIC ROCKET
CONTROL BOX
FANTASTICALLY DELICATE
DO NOT TOUCH

He had a good night's sleep and got up fairly early in order to connect up all the wires again. He didn't put them back exactly as he had found them, but he did think that his way was a big improvement, artistically speaking.

When he went to look in on his friends, he was surprised to find that they had been moved to a larger room which was full of people. The mayor and town councillors were there, making speeches, and there were lots of reporters taking notes. The mayor said proudly that Wortlethorpe would be the first borough council to put a mouse on the moon. Then the mayor's wife said that as chairwoman of the Wortlethorpe Ladies' Crocheting Society she could say that the ladies were behind him to a man because he was for Progress and without Progress there wouldn't be a single electric toothbrush or plastic hair-curler. After that, one of the scientists said that Arthur and Humphrey were the 20th-Century's Answer to Columbus and by going to the moon they were Planting Their Feet on the Threshold of a New Era. The two mice shouted that they would really much prefer to plant their feet on the threshold of Wortlethorpe Parish Church vestry and they couldn't possibly go to the moon because they hadn't left a note stopping the milk. But nobody listened to them.

Everybody was more interested in listening to the scientists, who were showing off the capsule in which the two mice would travel to the moon. They were particularly interested in the television camera which, the scientists said, would send back pictures of the moon and comets and things.

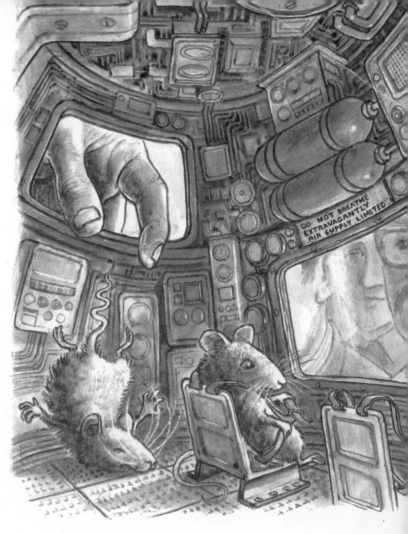

Then the mice were popped into the capsule and told to strap themselves in. A reporter asked how they were to get back from the moon, but the scientists pretended not to hear, and went on to say that blast-off was scheduled for 2·0000436 seconds after eleven, so there was just time for everybody to get a quick cup of tea.

When they'd finished their tea, the capsule, with Arthur and Humphrey inside it, was taken out to the launching pad. Everybody who was anybody in Wortlethorpe was there, hoping everything would go wrong.

When all was ready, one of the scientists looked at his watch. It had stopped, but he said it was probably somewhere around 2·0000436 seconds past eleven anyway, so the mayor might as well pull the firing handle.

It is very likely that Sampson's re-wiring had something to do with what happened next, but no one will ever know for sure.

When the rocket was at last out of sight, Sampson started to walk home. He felt sad because he thought he would never see his friends again and it had been nice having someone around to feel so superior to.

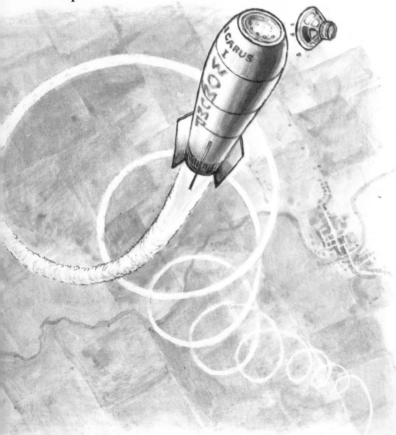

The two mice weren't feeling a bit sad. They were too busy feeling sick, frightened and dizzy. They kept their eyes tightly closed, and told each other in rather weak trembly voices that being an astronaut was really lovely.

Suddenly it seemed to go rather quiet, and after a few minutes there was a terrific splash, and everything came to an abrupt halt. And just at that very moment, Sampson reached the riverside path on his way home.

When the mice opened their eyes again, they thought they must have landed on the moon because a horrible monster was peering through the window at them.

But when the water had run off the glass, they saw that it was only Sampson, and they were so relieved that if they hadn't been trapped inside the capsule they would have given him a big kiss, even though he didn't like that kind of thing.

All the rest of the day they drifted slowly down-stream. Inside the capsule the two mice argued about whether or not the moon was further away than London, while outside, Sampson was wondering why poets were always writing poems about swans. But at last, just as the first stars were starting to show, Wortlethorpe church came into view around a bend. Sampson swam ashore and hurried to the vestry to round up the mice.

By the time the capsule came abreast of the church,
Sampson and the mice were ready and waiting.

Ever since blast-off, the two scientists had been trying
to make the TV set work so that they could see the
pictures the rocket was sending back to earth. They
had tried scientific methods, then they had kicked it,
and then they had shaken it, and then they had sworn
at it, and then they had discovered that it wasn't
plugged in. And by that time the capsule was ashore,
with its camera pointing at the sky, so the first thing the
scientists saw when they finally got the set going was a
picture of the moon. "The moon!" they cried
excitedly. "They're nearly there!"

Back at the church, Sampson had decided to drag the capsule into the vestry where there was light to see by as they worked to free Arthur and Humphrey.

And meanwhile the scientists' eyes were fixed on the TV screen. The next thing they saw would have made most people give up science forever. But when they had got over the shock, the two scientists agreed that they hadn't seen what they'd seen, because, if they had, it would prove that certain things existed which every good scientist knew jolly well didn't.

But they still had to go out and calm their nerves with a cup of instant coffee and a pork luncheon meat sandwich. And while they were doing this, Sampson and the mice dragged the capsule into the vestry and laid it on its side in order to get Arthur and Humphrey out. The TV camera in the capsule's nose now pointed straight at the mice's week's supply of cheese, brought for them by the parson that very morning.

When the scientists returned, the picture they saw on the TV screen filled them with joy. "We've done it!" they cried. "They've landed on the moon. Just look at those rocks, miles better than the silly old rocks that Apollo brought home."

Back in the vestry, the first thing that Arthur and Humphrey did on getting out of the capsule was to have a quick snack, even before they started bragging about being the first astronautical church mice in history. This nearly made the two scientists faint with delight. "It's edible!" they shrieked. "This is the greatest discovery since non-stick frying pans. Our names will rank with Newton and Darwin and Elvis Presley!"

They telephoned all the newspapers to tell them about their discovery, and they invited lots of reporters to come down next morning to see it for themselves on the TV set. The rest of the evening they spent arguing about which of them was the greatest scientist who had ever lived, but in the end they agreed that they both were. But never once did they spare a thought for the two mice whom they had bundled off into space, and who, as far as they knew, would spend the rest of their days twiddling their thumbs on the moon.

Next morning, after they had read all the nice things the newspapers had to say about them, they were, without doubt, the two happiest scientists in the world.

After breakfast, the scientists started to prepare the conference room, and they finished just as the reporters started arriving. They had all brought packed luncheons with them because they expected to be there a long time. By ten o'clock the room was full, and everyone waited eagerly for the mayor to switch the set on.

Meanwhile, back in the vestry, the capsule had been put to one side, out of the way, because things got pretty lively there on a Sunday just before the morning service began.

What they saw was much better than most things you see on the telly, but it just wasn't what everybody had been led to expect.

When there was complete silence in the conference room, the mayor made a few brief remarks about Man's Glorious Destiny and the Onward March of Knowledge, and then he solemnly switched on the TV, saying in a trembling voice, "Ladies and gentlemen of the press, behold, the moon."

The reporters were very angry indeed, and they put their packed luncheons to a use that was certainly never intended for them. Then they rushed off to write extremely nasty things about the mayor and town councillors of Wortlethorpe in their newspapers.

Then the mayor said things which can't be printed to the scientists, and the scientists said things which are best forgotten to the mayor, and the result of that was that the scientists were given their cards and five minutes to pack their bags and clear off the premises.

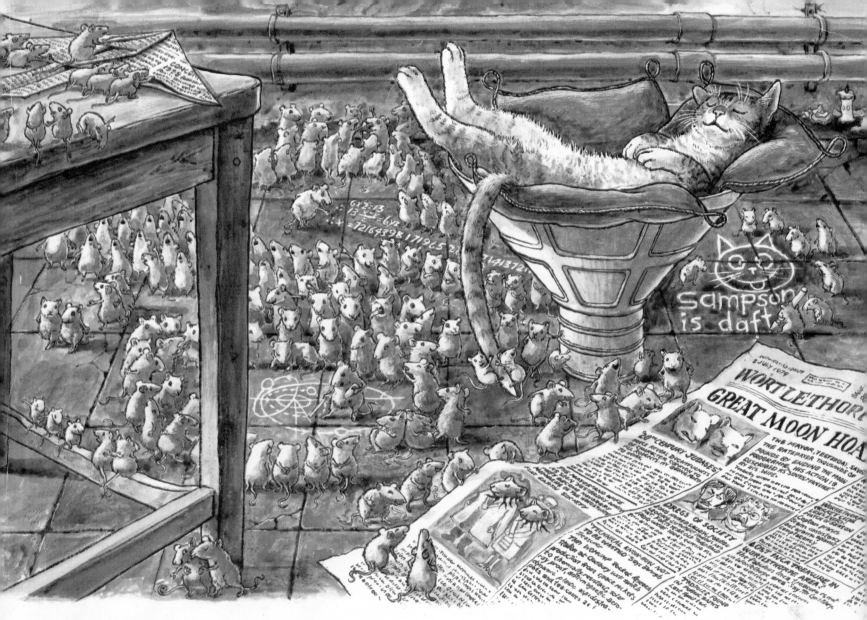

Some days later the mice and Sampson saw the two scientists again. Arthur and Humphrey were boring the fur off everybody with yarns about gravitational pull and computerized orbits, while Sampson had yet another forty winks, making a total of fifteen thousand, three hundred and twenty so far, and it was still only three o'clock, when a strange sound from the street brought everyone outside.

Now mice don't usually bear grudges, and, even though Arthur and Humphrey had been so abominably treated by the two men, they were really pleased to see them getting on in the world and doing something useful at last, instead of wasting their time playing with fireworks. Arthur even suggested borrowing a penny from the Save the Vestry Roof Fund collecting box to give them. But Humphrey, very sensibly, said that before giving the penny it would be best to wait until they could play something else besides the first two bars of *My Love is like a Red Red Rose*, otherwise they might think that success had come too easily, and stop trying.